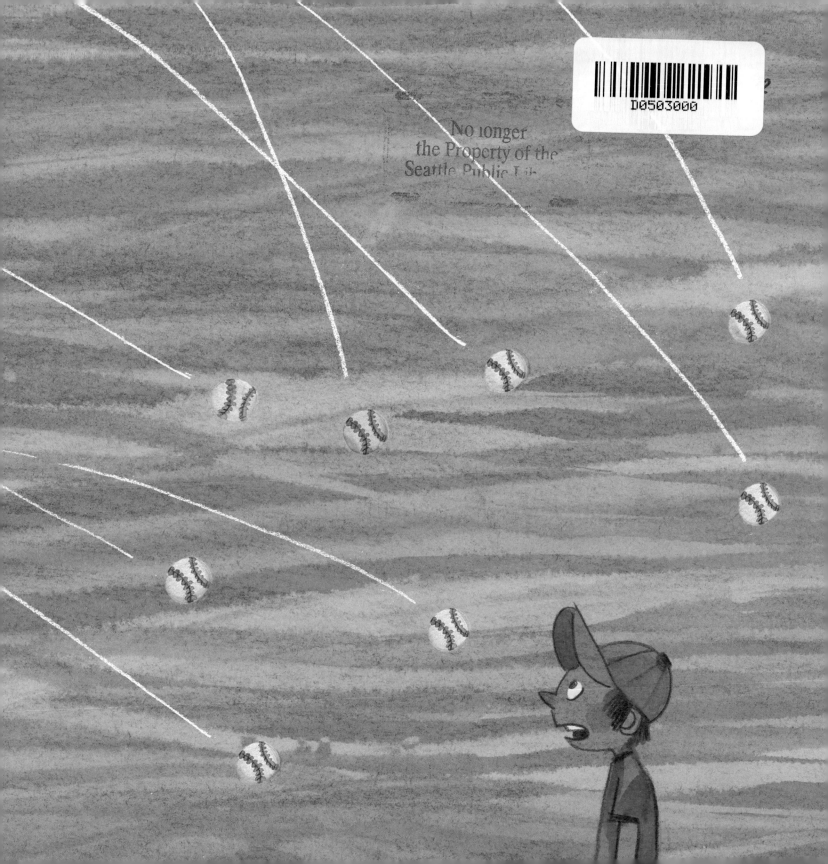

THE THING LENNY

LOVES MOST ABOUT

BASEBALL

For Charlie, you are the thing I love most about baseball.
With thanks to Toronto Playgrounds Baseball for fielding our dreams. — A.L.

To all young players out there who dream big — M.P.

Published in Canada and the U.S. by Kids Can Press Ltd.
25 Dockside Drive, Toronto, ON M5A 0B5

Kids Can Press is a Corus Entertainment Inc. company

www.kidscanpress.com

The artwork in this book was rendered on paper and digitally.
The text is set in Jansen.

Edited by Yvette Ghione
Designed by Marie Bartholomew

Printed and bound in Heyuan, China,
in 3/2021 by Asia Pacific Offset

CM 21 0 9 8 7 6 5 4 3 2 1

FSC
www.fsc.org
MIX
Paper from
responsible sources
FSC® C012521

Library and Archives Canada Cataloguing in Publication

Title: The thing Lenny loves most about baseball /
Andrew Larsen ; [illustrated by] Milan Pavlovic
Names: Larsen, Andrew, 1960- author. | Pavlovic Milan (Illustrator), illustrator.
Identifiers: Canadiana 20200226207 | ISBN 9781771389167 (hardcover)
Classification: LCC PS8623.A77 T55 2021 | DDC jC813/.6 — dc23

Kids Can Press gratefully acknowledges that the land on which our office is
located is the traditional territory of many nations, including the Mississaugas of
the Credit, the Anishnabeg, the Chippewa, the Haudenosaunee and the Wendat
peoples, and is now home to many diverse First Nations, Inuit and Métis peoples.

We thank the Government of Ontario, through Ontario Creates; the Ontario Arts
Council; the Canada Council for the Arts; and the Government of Canada for
supporting our publishing activity.

THE THING LENNY
LOVES MOST ABOUT
BASEBALL

ANDREW LARSEN   MILAN PAVLOVIC

KIDS CAN PRESS

There's a robin in the outfield. There's a kid on second base.

It's springtime at the park.

"One day I'm going to play in the big leagues," says Lenny, throwing the baseball.

"And I'll be there cheering for you," says his dad, catching it.

Later, Lenny looks through his *Big Book of Baseball Facts*. He thinks the more he knows, the better he'll play.

"Did you know a baseball game can go on and on and on?" he says. "It took the Pawtucket Red Sox and the Rochester Red Wings two whole days to play just one game!"

"That's a long game," says his dad.

"And it could have gone on forever," says Lenny. "I love that about baseball."

CRACK

It's the first game of the season.
Lenny is in the outfield.
   The batter blasts the ball with
a CRACK of the bat.
   Lenny tries to keep his eye on it.

He moves forward ...   Then backward ...   Then —

Lenny peeks out from behind his glove. The ball is on the grass by his feet.

"Maybe baseball isn't for me," says Lenny
on the walk home after the game.

"But you love baseball," says his dad.

"I love reading about it, but I'm not so good
at playing it," Lenny says. "I couldn't even
catch that pop fly."

"You just need to practice," says his dad.
"That's all."

That night, Lenny looks for more facts in his *Big Book of Baseball Facts*.

Babe Ruth: 714 career home runs, 1330 career strikeouts.

Hank Aaron: 755 career home runs, 1383 career strikeouts.

Babe Ruth and Hank Aaron were great players. They were all-stars. Hall of Famers! But they struck out more often than they hit home runs. They weren't great all the time.

I love that about baseball, thinks Lenny.

The next day, Lenny and his dad watch a game on television.

"Catchers are lucky," Lenny says. "They get to wear masks."

"They need the protection," says his dad.

"I have an idea," says Lenny. "Let's go to the park."

"What about the game?" says his dad.

"You said I need to practice!" says Lenny.

"Don't laugh," says Lenny, adjusting his helmet.

"Who's laughing?" says his dad. Then Lenny's dad throws the ball high into the air.

Lenny tries to keep his eye on it.

He moves to the right ...

Then to the left ...

Then —

The ball lands on the grass by Lenny's feet.
"Good try, Lenny!" says his dad. "Good try."
"Let's keep going," says Lenny.
Lenny catches a few. He misses a lot.
But he doesn't give up.

Lenny and his dad are back at the park the next morning.
"I'm ready to try without the helmet," says Lenny.
His dad tosses the ball high into the air.

Lenny keeps his eye on it.
He moves this way …
Then that way …
Then —

The ball lands snug in the pocket of Lenny's glove.
"Yesss!" says Lenny.

"Way to go, Lenny!" cheers his dad.
"Let's keep practicing," says Lenny with an
all-star smile. "I want to get good at this."

It's the second game of the season. Lenny is in the outfield.
It's the last inning.
The game is tied.
The other team's batter hits the first pitch.
Lenny keeps his eye on the ball.

He can tell where it's going.
And that's where Lenny goes.
He puts his glove high in the air.
Then —

The ball lands snug in the pocket of his glove.

"WAY TO GO, LENNY!" cheers his dad.
"Yesss!" his teammates call out. "Great catch, Lenny!"

The next batter comes up to the plate. She swings at the first pitch and misses. She swings at the second pitch and misses. She swings at the third pitch and —

CRACK!

The ball flies like a rocket!
It's going …
It's going …
It flies over Lenny's head … over
the fence … and into the trees.
IT. IS. GONE!
It's a home run!
Lenny has never played in a game
where the ball flies over the fence
and into the trees.

"Do you think I'll hit a home run some day?"
says Lenny on the way home after the game.
"If you keep swinging," says his dad.
"Did you see me catch that pop fly?"
"You were great."
"I felt like a real player!"
"You ARE a real player!" says his dad.

That night, Lenny looks at his *Big Book of Baseball Facts*. He wonders if one day he'll be in a book about baseball. He knows he can be great some of the time. And maybe that will be good enough.

That's the thing Lenny loves most about baseball.

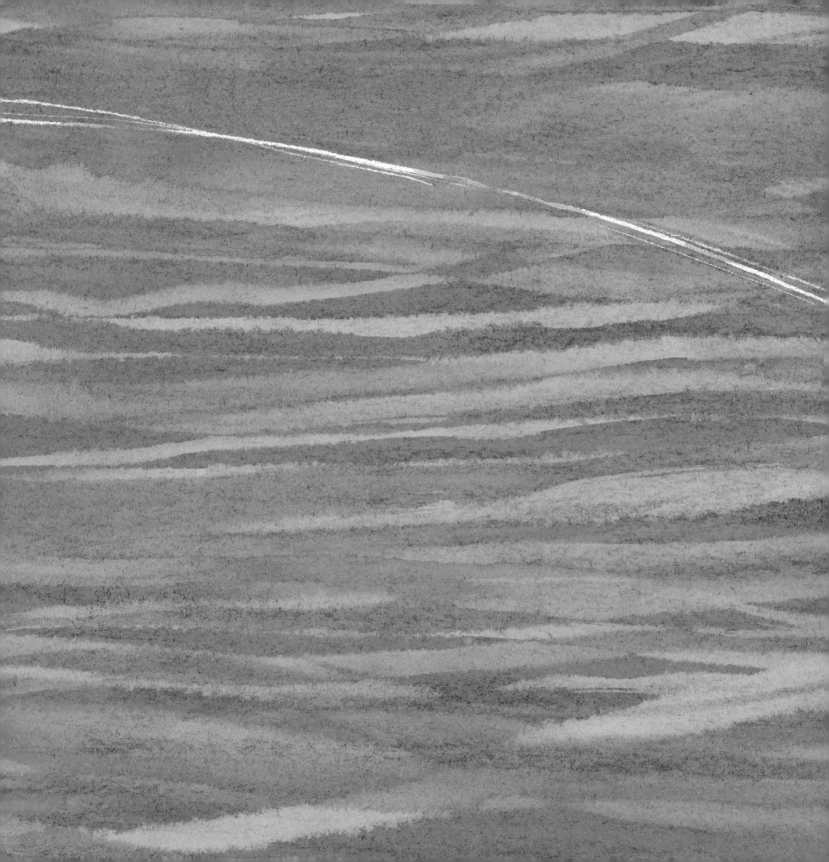